# Baby in Charge

adapted by **Maggie Testa**

**Simon Spotlight**
**New York London Toronto Sydney New Delhi**

SIMON SPOTLIGHT
An imprint of Simon & Schuster Children's Publishing Division
1230 Avenue of the Americas, New York, New York 10020
This Simon Spotlight paperback edition August 2019

For information about special discounts for bulk purchases, please contact Simon & Schuster Special Sales at 1-866-506-1949 or business@simonandschuster.com. Manufactured in the United States of America 0719 LAK
1 2 3 4 5 6 7 8 9 10 • ISBN 978-1-5344-5072-1 (pbk) • ISBN 978-1-5344-5073-8 (eBook)

Oh, hi there. Nice to meet you! Welcome to Baby Corp. Let's get down to business. My name is Boss Baby, but you can call me the Big Cheese. Or numero uno. Or just BB.

Around here I'm in charge. I'm the VP of field ops. My job keeps me pretty busy.

You might be asking yourself, what does a boss at Baby Corp. do all day? I will do anything I can to make sure baby love is at its highest—always. (*Even* if it means drinking milk out of a bowl and pretending I'm a kitten. Yup, I've done that!)

My field operations team of babies is the best of the best in this business or *any* business. They're always ready to do whatever is necessary to keep babies on top.

This is Staci. Staci might be the only baby who takes her job more seriously than I do. She has saved the day more times than I can count. She is very smart and she pretty much helps me run the show around here. Yeah, she'll be in charge one day.

This is Jimbo. Jimbo might *look* sweet and snuggly, but don't let his smile fool you—this baby brings the muscle in tough situations!

And here are the triplets. These three are always ready to help out. They don't always do their job very well, but these adorable babies always try!

At Baby Corp. we live by the rules of business. But family comes first, always. Even if they do make me wear a silly hat sometimes.

Meet Tim, my brother. Tim likes cookies and daydreaming and having fun. Oh, and he especially likes our family fun nights!

My brother is a wonderful member of my team. He doesn't know that much about business, so I'm teaching him as much as I can. He prefers just being a kid!

Here are my mom and dad. They don't know anything about Baby Corp. They are too busy planning fun activities for us to do as a family. They're really the best!

Business is important, but every night I make sure I’m home on time so I can have dinner with my family.

I even enjoy a round of Get That Baby every now and then! But if you tell anyone I said that, I will deny it. They'll think I'm going soft.

Recently, I had to save babies everywhere from the threat of kittens. Their human leader, Bootsy Calico, had been raised by kittens, and he was trying to cause a major *cat*-astrophe!

Bootsy Calico proved to
be quite a formidable,
feline-loving foe.

He got kittens to work together on his master plan,
but my trusty team and I succeeded in defeating him!

As long as I'm in charge, I promise that I will never rest—I'll even stay up all night if I have to—to make sure that babies get as much love as possible!

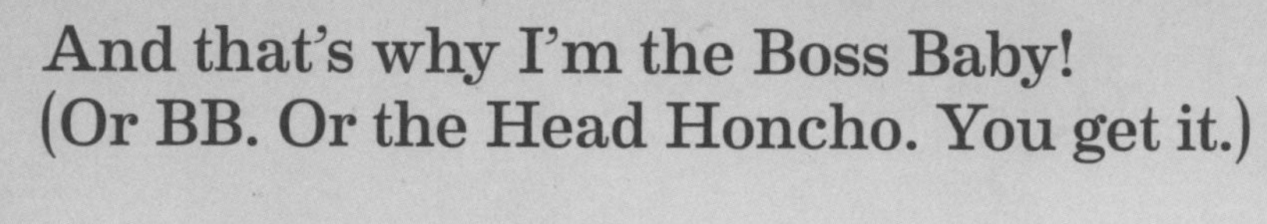

And that's why I'm the Boss Baby!
(Or BB. Or the Head Honcho. You get it.)